TULE REVIEW
2024

ACKNOWLEDGMENTS

Tule Review, founded in 1993, is published by The Sacramento Poetry Center, a not-for-profit, tax-exempt organization registered in the State of California, and funded through our memberships, public donations, and the Sacramento Office of Arts and Culture. Contributions to SPC are appreciated and tax-deductible.

Editor-In-Chief: Linda Jackson Collins
Managing Editor: Patrick Grizzell

Cover art: *Honey Comb*, mixed media painting © 2024, by Donna D. Vitucci. Final cover layout by Liz Ryder Baxmeyer

Publishing Credits:

Prophecy of the Trees, by Mary Mackey, will appear in her upcoming collection titled In *This Burning World* (Marsh Hawk Press).

Sandra Rendig's poems will appear in her forthcoming collection, *Heart and Bones*, from The Poetry Box.

The Blue Hour, by Ann Wehrman, was previously published in *Medusa's Kitchen*.

TULE REVIEW 2024 © 2024 / ISBN 9798340600233
Authors and artists maintain copyright of their work.

The Sacramento Poetry Center
1719 25th Street
Sacramento, California 95816
sacpoetrycenter.org

TULE REVIEW

2024

Editor-in-Chief
Linda Jackson Collins

Cover Artist
Donna D. Vitucci

Published by The Sacramento Poetry Center Press
1719 25th Street
Sacramento, California, 95816

sacpoetrycenter.org

In Memoriam Sandra McPherson
(August 2, 1943 - August 19, 2024)

This issue of Tule Review is dedicated to the memory of Sandra McPherson, a beloved and much celebrated poet who passed away in Davis, California on August 19, 2024. Sandy was a mentor and guide to many, always doing whatever she could to cast more light on poetry and poets.

RIP dear Sandy.

Poppies

Orange is the single-hearted color. I remember
How I found them in a vein beside the railroad,
A bumble-bee fumbling for a foothold
While the poppies' petals flagged beneath his boot.

I brought three poppies home and two buds still sheathed.
I amputated them above the root. They lived on artlessly
Beside the window for a while, blazing orange, bearing me
No malice. Each four-fanned surface opened

To the light. They were bright as any orange grove.
I watched them day and night stretch open and tuck shut
With no roots to grip, like laboratory frogs' legs twitching
Or like red beheaded hens still hopping on sheer nerves.

On the third afternoon one bud tore off its green glove
And burst out brazen as Baby New Year.
Two other poppies dropped their petals, leaving four
Scribbly yellow streamers on a purple-brimmed and green

Conical cadaver like a New Year's hat.
I'd meant to celebrate with them, but they seemed
So suddenly tired, these aging ladies in crocheted
Shawl leaves. They'd once been golden as the streets

Of heaven, now they were as hollow.
They couldn't pull together for a last good-bye.
I had outlived them and had only their letters to read,
Fallen around the vase, saying they were sorry.

From *Elegies for the Hot Season* by Sandra McPherson. (The Ecco Press, 1970)

INTRODUCTION

With this issue of *Tule Review,* the Sacramento Poetry Center continues its tradition of showcasing fine poetry from both new and familiar voices. In these pages you'll find writing from as far away as Kazakhstan and as close as V Street, Sacramento. Yet these poems transcend physical and cultural distance in how they evoke human strengths and frailties, and in their observations about our beautiful, but vulnerable, earth. After spending time with the many wonderful submissions we received, I can't help but feel optimistic that our shared humanity will overcome our differences. It has been an honor to assemble this collection and be reminded that

> *Distance between us*
> *narrows, then widens*
> *and narrows again.*

— Linda Jackson Collins, Editor

(lines from Sue Daly's poem, *Like shooting stars*)

TABLE OF CONTENTS

Introduction ix

Karen DeFoe 1
    The Cellist

Matthew J. Andrews 2
    Delta
    Metamorphosis

Paul Aponte 4
    El Sol
    The Sun

Catherine Arra 6
    Like This Hazy, Hard-to-See-the-Horizon Day
    Garniture of Grief

John Bell 8
    The Hawks

Lynn Belzer 9
    The Cool Land Park Bus

Catherine Bridge 10
    The Chinese Magnolia Spins By

Katy Brown 11
    painted faces

John Allen Cann 12
    Afterview

Lucille Lang Day   13
    Busan: Headong Yonggungsa Temple

Sharon Coleman   14
    stroke
    trestles

Sue Daly   16
    Like shooting stars
    The Other Side of Winter

Tino De Guevara   18
    Dragoness

Cindy Domasky   19
    Leaving Guilt Behind

Bob Eakins   20
    Last Time Home
    Quarry Water

Mary Eichbauer   22
    Lemon Solstice
    Pataphysics

Susan Flynn   24
    Still

Laura Garfinkel   25
    Takotsubo Cardiomyopathy,
        also known as Broken Heart Syndrome

Callie Goff 26
    Before Hospice
    To Persephone, Whose Head Hangs

Dr. Jeremy DeWayne Greene 28
    Who We Are

Anara Guard 30
    A Handful of Reasons

Tom Goff 32
    At Empire Mine State Park

Jan Haag 33
    Groceries

David Holper 34
    Working Within A Form

Diana MacKinnon Henning 35
    Easy To Miss Something Small

Jocelyn Heath 36
    Memory Garden
    Forward Motion

Sibilla Hershey 38
    Night Train

Connie Johnstone 39
    Hell's Kitchen

Anthony Xavier Jackson 40
    Famine

Nora Laila Goff   43
    The Basil Can Save Us

Andy Jones   44
    Babassu Fronds

Jane Rosenberg LaForge   45
    Haunted Mansion

Mary Mackey   46
    Prophecy of the Trees

Melisa McCampbell   47
    Pruners' Code

Moira Magneson   48
    Two Weeks into the New Administration
    Half-Life

Rita Fuhr Marowitz   50
    Hard Lessons

Deborah Melvedt   52
    Apology
    When they ask you what you like about your body
        and all you can say is my collarbones

Ann Michaels   54
    Daughters Dreaming in the Bones of an Absent Father

Casey Mills   56
    Home State
    In the End

MLuv   58
    The Process

Ebony Patiño   59
    I am a Whoaman

Jennifer O'Neill Pickering   60
    First Star on the First Night of the New Year

Shawn Pittard   62
    Thin Places

Danyen Powell   63
    Lake Tahoe at Noon

Ross Powers   64
    Unhoused

Rick Rayburn   65
    The Fresno Poet

Sandra Rendig   66
    Hour Of Dancing Wings
    Sweet Grief

Melinda Rivasplata   68
    All The Colors You Can Feel

Allegra Silberstein   69
    A gravel road

Yuriy Serebriansky   70
    Ашаршылық
    Asharshylyq

Don Solomon 72
    Climbing Butcher Hill
    Insomnia 3:04 a.m.

Bob Stanley 74
    Where It Needs to Be

Jeanine Stevens 75
    Tule Elk

Alex Stolis 76
    Into the Land

Gary Thomas 77
    Sunshine on the Giant Orange

Ziaeddin Torabi 78
    Hanging Gardens

Ann Wehrman 79
    January in Sacramento
    The Blue Hour

Patricia Wentzel 80
    The Beckoning Bed

Wendy Williams 82
    Where Hawks Fly
    Early Mornings

Nanci Woody 84
    A Sweeter Gift

Andrena Zawinski   85
    When I was just a kid.

Stan Zumbiel   86
    The Sea Calls Me Back
    Bird First for Joy

Contributors   88

Karen DeFoe

The Cellist

Sitting on his stool,
knees wide apart, he
embraces his instrument
like a dancer joins his partner in
a sensual pas de deux,
his left hand holding it
close to his chest, guiding
its elegant neck to rest
upon his shoulder,
his right hand, fingers extended,
drawing the rosined bow
across taut strings.

The throaty timbre vibrates,
smooth honeyed hums,
a precious elixir of sounds
like liquid amber poured
from a priceless urn,
slowly infusing the air with
sustained richness, ripe
mellow tones, gliding, swelling,
rolling over and over, enticing
the imagination,
heightening the senses,

the glow of a fiery sunset,
the warmth of apricot brandy
on a crisp autumn evening.

Matthew J. Andrews

Delta

1.

Last year it was campers on the shoreline,
dotting each island like fleas.
By day, jet skis and fishing reels;

at night, drunken songs by the fire,
laughter rising into the darkness
like a burning that may never cease.

2.

This year, a whale lost its way, trapped
in the suburban labyrinth of halting river.
Home receding in memory, its skin

grew ashen, its swimming decayed
to a slow eddy, its song grew heavier,
the music sinking to the muddy depths.

3.

Next year, I will take the kayak and paddle
aimlessly, giving myself fully to the dance
of current and salt. There will be smoke, surely.

Embers like tiny stars. And silence,
or close to it, the slurping strain of dirt
the only melody left in my ears.

Metamorphosis

She begins to collect birds
along her outstretched arms
until the skin is covered in plumage.

In the latitude of darkness,
she pecks at my neck,
digs her fingers into my thigh.

We paint the walls green,
the ceiling blue. I scatter
leaves at the foot of the bed.

She takes on colors: deep scarlets
and sunset yellows, a shimmering
in the breast that leaves me in awe.

The sky opens and she soars for hours
overhead, so majestic as she swirls.
I stand in the grass and hold out my arms.

Paul Aponte

El Sol

En un Sueño —
Un hogar extraño y familiar.
Un amor ... extraño y familiar.
Ondulaciones rítmicas y apasionadas.

El sol refleja en el fondo de mi despertar
y el sueño desvanece en deseos.
Una ardilla corre sobre el cerco.
Miro el reloj acelerar mi cerebro.
Esta ardilla comienza su ronda.

Café y reflejos.
El espejo inevitable.
La percepción. Las calculaciones.
El cerillo se transforma sobre el raspador.

El hacer, rehacer, quehacer,
buen hacer del hacer.
El responsable hacer.
El hacer para hacer,
y la vida se hace.

La vida
hace vida.
Y al anochecer
vives y vivo.

Y recuerdo mi sueño,
y soñamos juntos.

The Sun

In a dream —
A strange yet familiar home.
A love ... strange and familiar.
Rhythmic and passionate undulations.

The sun reflects in the background of my awakening
and the dream fades into desires.
A squirrel runs along the fence.
I see the clock speed up my brain.
This squirrel begins his rounds.

Coffee and reflections.
The unavoidable mirror.
Perceptions. Calculations.
The match transforming on the striking surface.
Doing, redoing, undoing,
the good doing of doing.
The responsible deeds.
The doing just to do,
and life is made.
Life
livens life.
And at night
you live and I live.

And I remember my dream,
and we dream together.

(Translated by the author.)

Catherine Arra

Like This Hazy, Hard-to-See-the-Horizon Day

I'm muddled as weather. Squint into clouds
to define illusion, trace the figure with a sleight of hand,
side tricks, mirrored distortions, desire, piqued and sated
in a disheveled bed, unrequited dreams

to define illusion, trace the figure with a sleight of hand,
I find him in fog, a decloaked magician floundering
in a disheveled bed, unrequited dreams
in a roaring river, torrents slapping his face, his plight.

I find him in fog, a decloaked magician floundering
voiceless against churning eddies, rolling rapids
in a roaring river, torrents slapping his face, his plight.
He can't swim. Panics

voiceless against churning eddies, rolling rapids.
He manifests a death story
in a roaring river, torrents slapping his face, his plight.
His fear is not my fear. His story not my story.

He manifests a death story
I walk from shore to forest. Leave him to find his way.
His fear is not my fear. His story not my story.
I've crossed this river, alone, and know

I walk from shore to forest. Leave him to find his way.
I cannot save him.
I've crossed this river, alone, and know
I cannot save him.

Garniture of Grief

Fighting conch, lightning welk,
calico clams, angel wings, coquina

> bellies gutted, crowns clipped, spikes shorn
> smooth, wave sculpted in iridescent sheens.

Tumbling in foam and sand, salty,
I rescue each as if a wounded seabird,

> bucket my bounty home, flush embedded
> grit, leaving tiny shells swirled into curves.

On the porch ledge, they remind me
no matter how rugged the armor,

> how sharp the edges, the life inside is fragile.
> Everything breaks.

Pieces float in tides, wash ashore, recede,
tumble back in the diastole and systole.

John Bell

The Hawks

Highway in eastern Kansas
        Red-tailed hawks on patrol
    Wheat, corn, beans, millet
        Rodents to catch
            Until the farms become subdivisions
        More Mercedes than mule deer
      More malamutes than mice
  Raptors moving on

        Freeway in California
      Middle of a suburb
        Next to a park with
              Horses and mews
          Stables and hay
            A riding club there
         Since the Spanish ruled
      Hawks patrol the exit
  Mice don't get away

Lynn Belzer

The Cool Land Park Bus

> *Dinner is a casual affair.*
> *Two who are Mostly Good.*
> *Two who have lived their day*
> — The Bean Eaters, Gwendolyn Brooks

I see the elderly couple smiling, eating dinner
at a worn wooden table which is
within their nomadic home, a
vintage regulation-size yellow school bus, casual
creative, perfect for their 50+ years-long love affair.

If they were in 1960's San Francisco I might have seen these two
among the myriad of brightly dressed young couples who
joined protests, smoked weed, attended concerts at the Fillmore and are
now still passionate and engaged, mostly
upright, liberal and involved in causes that are good.

Grey-haired and tanned, these two
often park near the perennial garden, among people who
hire and welcome them, have
admired their solar features, how they've lived
their dream, and their
charisma in our community each day.

Catherine Bridge

The Chinese Magnolia Spins By

A framed still life on a Sunday morning —
this window with its spill of leaves,
a motionless cascade of green ears, tongues

divided by the casement squares,
a modest backlit green on creamy stucco,
gilded still life on a Sunday morning.

The clock ticks, some bacterium engulfs
another, plaque goes on closing an artery —
outside, a motionless cascade of green ears, tongues

looms lighter, larger than the pictures framed inside
though just as still while all's in flux...
a framed still life on a Sunday morning.

The floorboards creak, the traffic sighs, something with
blood pumping through a heart moves out of frame,
still, that motionless cascade of green ears, tongues.

Watcher and watched balance on this spinning place
where leaves and flesh get conjured somehow from the orbit light
to make a framed still life on a Sunday morning,
a motionless cascade of green ears, tongues.

Katy Brown

painted faces

never doubt the wilderness in women
the savage incantation
the primal dream of pure desire

they learned to spin
from cave orbs, mythic spiders
with webs that capture dreams

they gather herbs for murky purpose
under the dark of the moon
and simmer them in ancient cauldrons

wild women paint their faces
with lines of power
they chant starlight and firelight

when they walk at night
a darker shadow goes before them
to summon owl and raven

they exhale moths and fireflies —
they witch the water from barren ground
never doubt the wilderness in women

John Allen Cann

Afterview

It's possible you may disbelieve
my catching sight of Rilke's ghost

in the shadows of Hopper's world,
savoring a kind of urban solitude

we've come to call American.
Rilke has just left the Nighthawk Café,

beside his empty cup, a rose for a tip.
He appreciates that even when sunlit,

this world still is dark, streets are empty,
storefronts blank, & it's best to look

in a window if you want to see how solitary
people really are, even with someone else.

Wrapped in his own solitude, Rilke
feels right at home; he's always been careful

to stay far from anyone close to him. Alone,
he looks for Hopper in a movie theater,

half-full of people sitting apart
watching a love story set in Paris.

Later, chauffeured by Death in a classic Ford,
he rides silent roads past the uncanny faces

of Victorian houses, through vacant hills,
until he's dropped off at a lighthouse

on the windless Coast of Privacy. Nearby
in the keeper's house, he studies long

how the light falls on the wall
of an empty room,

before he begins to write about it
in the little notebook he always carries with him.

Lucille Lang Day

Busan: Headong Yonggungsa Temple

The twelve animals of the Chinese
zodiac line up to guard the gate.
I was born in a Year of the Pig,
a symbol of wealth and abundance.

I would share my abundance
with children stunted by malnutrition
in Yemen, their food taken away
by Iranian-backed Houthi rebels.

And also with the starving millions
in the Democratic Republic of Congo,
Afghanistan, Syria, the Sahel,
Somalia, Ethiopia, Sudan, and Gaza.

Facing the Buddha for Academic
Achievement, I make a request:
marinated pork for students in Haiti,
along with soup and good grades.

Sixteen baby buddhas on a ledge:
Thirteen sit. One reclines. One sleeps.
One prays. A woman bows her head.
May great abundance begin today.

Sharon Coleman

stroke

        the yellow orchid
petals   have grown
camouflaged   twisted
high   among the house
plants   that vine
across   the front
window   a chlorophyl
curtain between sidewalk
street and   my mother's
left hand   its fingers now
useless under her right —
five pale petals   reddish
tongue   white nose
disks   enmeshed
in curvilinear   greens
to support heavy blooms
it's a week before I notice
some days   before I ask
she says   she put them
there   with stems high
curving over each flower
facing   a different
way   so nobody
would notice

trestles

rain   after the rains
grayed water   sky hills
this bridge   so open
just lanes   bisecting
salt beds   waiting birds
every molecule of oxygen
colliding   with cloud
breath   above
a green-gray   bay
horizon's   inky line
thick and steady between
hands holding the wheel

this bridge   so long
length   of my mother's
dying   her swallow again
giving up   swish-swash
of a heartbeat   we were
waiting for sun   i scan
the blue hills   behind
her home   a skyline
thickened   by light rain
ending   our drought

Sue Daly

Like shooting stars

we burn through
the atmosphere.
Disappointed clouds
pull us higher —
we soar through them
like identical twins.
We glide side by side
in dark space,
deep space —
pass through nebulas
and nonsense, try to
choose one or the other.
Distance between us
narrows, then widens
and narrows again.
Time mirrors us together
as we dance —
like shooting stars.

The Other Side of Winter

She grants her grace once more.
Miniature buds command bitter
skies to vanish, announcing —
Your services are no longer required.

Our Lady of Spring unmasks her face,
tinged with a gilded glow.
Jasmine breezes begin to blow
the mourning clouds away.

We'll trudge this trail for now —
pretend the other side of Winter
is just out of sight, a little up ahead,
a stone's throw away.

Tino De Guevara

Dragoness

Baby, you've got nails
Like a Chinese Dragon
Colorful, long and deadly.
You can use them
To etch your initials
On my back, pick door locks
And summon hapless sailors onto your shores
Manicuring Asian maidens admire them
Purring like a sultry feline

Men look at them in awe
Remembering that time
In Yokohama, on-shore leave
And the exotic girls
At the Shitty Kitty Dance Club
Who caressed the inside of their thighs
With tantalizing pleasure

I shiver when
You run them through my hair
Vamping me like Brigette Bardot
Or Marilyn Monroe.
Don't ever cut them
Paint them
Like the totems in Ketchikan
Like the Northern Lights
In the far cold reaches
Of my blue jean breeches

Cindy Domasky

Leaving Guilt Behind

> *for my daughter, Christie*
> *December 26, 1976 – September 3, 2023*

I finally put up the bird feeder.
I love watching the finches flit in and out,
sometimes bumping into one another,
Sometimes hovering — almost like hummingbirds —
wings opened.
The seeds are everywhere.
Such gluttons.

What speaks to them when they hurry off?
It doesn't matter —
watching them is enough.
Some secrets of the universe
deserve to remain a mystery.

Bob Eakins

Last Time Home

My father says he wants to *amble* —
as though the word is archaic, foreign.

His steps are mostly aimless along sidewalks
cracked and angled to catch the tip of his cane

while he leans on my shoulder with his free
hand. In front of his boyhood home, he notes

the height of maple trees he and his mother
planted, the worn patches of lawn he mowed,

where he and his sister chased decoy killdeer.
At the Motel 6 this morning he said

this is his last time home, that all blood
must be new at some point, that even the deepest,

oldest wounds must be freshly skinned over.
We let July's humidity press us.

Turning, he keeps his hand on my shoulder
as we walk to the car, and when his fingers

tighten into my own skin I wonder about
where he bled, how he was wounded.

Quarry Water

The brave among us submerged into
legends of the dead. In water cold
enough to hold its sons for generations

of grief, we imagined their final,
hopeless struggles against cramps
and strands of cable our grandfathers

left behind. Willie, the minister's son,
said drowning was for the unbaptized,
the unwashed souls who beckoned us

always deeper. The brave, the meek — we all
believed him then. We believed in God's
choices, in better places, in the day

when each drowned boy would break
the surface and rejoice.

Mary Eichbauer

Lemon Solstice

After Eugenio Montale

It's that golden hour when the sun lies down
and sweeps the land with brassy light
that pulls the lemons out among the leaves
and shows us what they are

Then the sun falls behind that first hill
and darkness floods the air
with blue from a saturated paintbrush,
rippling across the stone path,
dimming the purple salvia to wine

I wish I could paint the exact shade of blue
that eclipses the leaves,
the slight breeze that moves them,
flattening clouds at the horizon
into woolly streaks

As day abandons us,
yellow leaves wrinkle into brown
against the fog-wrapped hills,
leaving in our mouths
the sour note of unripe fruit

While the lemons keep on glowing
with their own internal light
by day, by night,
growing sunnier in the mind,
sweet as flame to winter eyes

Pataphysics

She doesn't know what will happen in Barcelona,
among the spiring churches, the winding streets
that lead to markets, or squares, or cobbled ways
that give no clue to who lives there
or where they are on this sullen afternoon.

Why has she come here? She doesn't know
the uses of the city, the footfalls that have padded,
that will whisper past, passions that have worn
the stones smooth, the leather soles that pinch

as poetry sometimes pinches, when our feet
don't fit their shoes, when we miss our footing
in the unknown city, staring at a torn poster,
a grinning clown torn through one eye
with a woman underneath, or half a woman,

as if the wall were a limpid pool, a profundity
that promises to heal the ruptured self,
if only we would lift our feet, walk briskly,
prance, strike sparks with nail-studded heels,
tempting words to fly up from stones,
discovering a whole new way to go.

Susan Flynn

Still

> *And night is night*
> *I am not deceived, I do not think it is still summer*
> *Because sun stays and birds continue to sing.*
> — Gwendolyn Brooks

It is December, and
shadows lean toward night.
Quiet, dense silence is
all around me tonight.
Friends are busy. I
am often alone. I am
still, often happy. Not
much to do. Not deceived
by sparkly things, my days have slowed. I
welcome sun's slippage, return. Do
necessary things, not
too many. I think
often of swimming in Michigan. It
is memory that calms me. It is
memory that soothes. Still,
moments beckon. Not summer,
not tomorrow. Light falls, because
it's time. Sun
rises. The morning stays
ready, a window just open, and
the birds, bless those birds,
they always continue
                to
                      sing

Laura Garfinkel

Takotsubo Cardiomyopathy,
also known as *Broken Heart Syndrome*

The Octopus — den seeker, container nester,
creature of the dark. Just wants to hide.

When she hits the surface, does she surge with stress
pulsating within her walls, stunned from comfort,

home and rest. Chest tightness, chills,
dizzy, shortness of breath.

The Mother, eye of the storm, glue that holds family —
carer, sharer, wearer on the sleeve, the go-to-get-it-done-er,

problem solver, tear dissolver, issue resolver. Her
left ventricle swells to look like the fishing pot.

This fragile ticker needs tender care and healing
to regain normal rhythm, steady beats. For now,

my darlings, no more fishing in these seas.

> This syndrome is named after Japanese ceramic pots used
> by fisherman to trap Octopus. The heart's left ventricle,
> flooded with stress hormone, swells to look like one of these
> Tako-tsubo vessels.

Callie Goff

Before Hospice

Dorothy dressed in a simple cross and
cigarette smoke, caught
gnats at the dinette between her
pointer finger and thumb while humming
birds pecked at the window to beg for her
gentle attention.
When she drifted away from me and sang
sweetly to fill bright red bottles with sugarwater,
it seemed as if the rotted wood would
straighten instead of sag, and bloom
with butterfly weed within every gap.
But I remember only decay — the way that each porch step
threatened with buckles and
creaks, or how the swing screamed under her light
weight, despite how she had sunken into herself
like limestone.
Why can't you sing again, why can't you
sing?

To Persephone, Whose Head Hangs

like the yellow narcissus I pluck from loamy
soil the second it springs — the same way he
emerged from a fissure in the earth
to pull you beyond the roots
into warm arms. Do you remember the lure
of those vibrant petals, pushed outward and opening
themselves wider and wider as if to dare you to desire
their delicate edges and cup
a gentle form that did not ask
for your palms to warp
and rip
from home.
Just a girl then, you clasped
your small hands tight around the cruelty
that surrounds beauty before descending
underground, burning every last
perianth brown.
Up here, they freeze.
Not only when you leave,
but when you are the only bulb to bloom
in a sea of blind stems. This must be why you hang
your head downward and wish to be
swallowed up again every spring.
Is there no place you can settle in?
I wonder if this is what it means to become
a woman.

Dr. Jeremy DeWayne Greene

Who We Are

for the UOP Black Grad Class of 2024

Who are we?
We are the chosen.
The talented truth.
The constant rotation
in which the universe moves.

We are justice seekers.
Hardly people pleasers.
We have survived millennia
to reach this point of
education while still
advocating for salvation.

Who we are cannot
be defined by
privileged minds.
It cannot be stereotyped
by those who fear our genius.
By those who claim they
"keep the peace" by attempting
to silence our soul.
They cannot destroy
what is rooted in
the cosmic design.

Who we are is beyond
any social construction.
Beyond propaganda.
Beyond Ivory Towers
that house those who are
as transparent as
the glass they
throw stones through.

For we have been constructed
with the universal.
The cosmic design which exists
within each helix coil
of our DNA.

It is within these
unseen strands where
our mind is capable
of producing dreams
in real time.

They can never take our shine.
They can never take our hope.
They can never take our dreams.
They will never take our soul.

Who we are has
survived and energized
multiple lifetimes.

Even in the midst of chaos
we still thrive.

Even with the weight
of the world within our chest
still, we rise.

Who we are is the truth that
they cannot define nor deny.

Let the ancestors' dreams
continue to provide through
this lifetime…

The light that we be.

Anara Guard

A Handful of Reasons

    I.   because the funeral

You let go of my hand to speak,
wanting to correct the old men
in their black and orange college colors
as they swapped stories
of his wit and acumen.
When I was a boy, you said,
My father washed my mouth out with soap.
The irony escaped you,
but his friends knew those efforts
to teach you proper speech
had been lost,
dissolved upon your tongue.

    II.   because the motel

After a weekend of dancing on the beach,
before we left that cheap Florida motel —
their swimming pool filled with sand,
sign blown down by a hurricane —
you stripped our room bare.
You took the teabags and coffee packets,
all the wooden stirrers and Styrofoam cups,
artificial creamer you would never drink.
Why not? We paid for it, you said as you packed
the little bottles of shampoo, lotion,
conditioner, the tiny bars of soap,
a blue plastic shower cap.
Tissues. The dry cleaning bag.
Only Gideon's Bible remained in its drawer.
You carried your suitcase to the car;
I went back, wondering
if the tip I'd left for the maid
remained on the vanity.

    III.   because the things

Despite your delicate touch,
the masseur's gifted hands, you scorched

my best pan and snapped
the kayak's rudder in a tangle of river weeds.
Borrowed my watch and lost it.
Dropped your phone into water.
Blew out a tire by hitting the curb
on three different occasions.
I wept over something you broke
but now can't remember
which beloved cup or bowl
lay in pieces, only my grief.

    IV.   because the clock

Too lively for deadlines,
you were late to dinner
and to so many dates,
always running behind,
bills overdue,
debt collectors on the phone.
I learned to arrive alone
and if asked when to expect you
to bound in, ever exuberant,
all I could do was shrug.

    V.   because the words

The couples counselor's assignment:
write two pages about yourself.
You brought twenty looseleaf papers —
so much to say and still not done.
You carried every grudge
as if tattooed on your heart:
baby of the family, always left out.
Unpaid loans. Your bankruptcy.
The unfair custody arrangement.
And at the very end,
as you cursed me,
I remembered your father's
useless bar of soap.

Tom Goff

At Empire Mine State Park

Again we amble about through June day heat
On delicately graveled walks we walked
Twenty-eight years ago. Footsore cops, beat
Unchanged, don't know it like we know this terrain, stalked
With rose exotics and dark Italian cypress:
One planting, to symbolize bud-bursting life;
One green-black, giraffe-tall, dares us to bypass…
We stride ahead, husband to husband, wife to wife;
Bugloss, Sombreuils & red climbing rose vines.
Overlaps of sun-shadow — déjà vu
Makes blends of us, Venn diagrams of us. Light outlines
My silhouette, your profile. Sun-tinged, we two
Tread grasses, thread hedges. Mine-gold to delve for? Day
Of Return: Butterflies, new & bygone, vows we still say.

Jan Haag

Groceries

We all bear the great weight
of unseen somethings.

For you, one hand hovering over
the avocados, carrying the great grief

of *how could that happen?*
that wasn't supposed to happen.

For her, pushing the dense
boulder of a shopping cart

seemingly uphill, filled with
if only, if only, if only.

For him, picking up the quart
of milk, then the remembering,

the putting it back of *how*
could you leave me like this?

For me, filling a bag with
loose-leaf tenderness,

along with a handful
of softheartedness,

and leaving it right there
for you, for her, for him,

to lighten the heaviness
of the invisibles we tote,

everywhere we go.

David Holper

Working Within A Form

There is a tension in the form
that forms a tension in the line
that speaks to how you choose a word

or cut one free — to simplify.
There is a tension in a life
living within this sense of form

and having it, you work within
what bounds your days
between sun and shade,

making you choose with care
what will and will not suffice.
And thus, you choose

a form and fashion well:
so when you're done,
the scars won't tell.

Diana MacKinnon Henning

Easy To Miss Something Small

A ball of feathers snugs the cinder blocks of my guest cabin,
round and plump and when I turn the clump over,
it's a sparrow, hazy eyes already disappearing

like The Father seldom present,
who faded into whiskey's distance,
his black lunch pail a miniature coffin
carried on a chain of regret.

*Listen up, you've wasted years on your father,
stay with the bird* you tell yourself.

A miscalculation, knocked dead against the window,
what I surmise happened to this sparrow
that rests in the cradle of my shovel.

It was also judgement's error when Father
barreled through *Woolworth's* display window,
drunk on Jack Daniels.

Now, where to put my small God —
out to sun, or on freshly fallen oak leaves
so my sparrow might become a tree.

Jocelyn Heath

Memory Garden

> "Designed to meet the special needs of those
> with memory disorders (such as Alzheimer's disease)...
> [with] plants and flowers in raised beds that have been
> chosen to stimulate the senses and to spark past memories."
> — Portland Memory Garden

Your hand opens, warms on granite, reaches
now for clustered tulips the yellow

of rubber, of ducks and raincoats —
of painted tin toy trucks

banging down the hills of The Hollow,
with the boys' knees tearing across pavement

and the red rush of poppies
from planters, for armistice

drained of color in newsprint
to the white of asters;

soft eyelash fringe of a sleeping son,
of the false or mascara-thick

batting at steelmillers in the dance hall,
while your brother glowers from the bar —

crook of fingers on a wedding day,
held and beholden

under a gold cross, a blue dome
the shade of forget-me-not or violet,

shade of shaggy pines
over baseballs and grandchildren

on blue June evenings,
cigarettes and roses and paint

flaking from railings onto grass,
like slate flagstones

shape this circle that
you walk for hours.

Forward Motion

My knees whiten; his turn flush,
skin dragged against the carpet in a rush
to intercept hands grabbing a cat, a crumb
of day-old bread, a glass. My thumb
the length of his hand for now,
there's no sure way of telling how
long till his fingers pass mine in reach —
or when his excited screech
will turn to shrieks of discontent.
Once he has the speed to circumvent
me, he'll move ever farther to explore
the lake, a tree, turtles on the shore,
oblivious to his mother's concern.
Things once known, we can't unlearn.

Sibilla Hershey

Night Train

Snow had fallen
on the North China Plain
a world without maps
or familiar landmarks
white borderless silence
where ghosts walk on tiptoe
and disappear behind
a carved screen.
We were two
riding in the dark
sharing a light.
Under the silk quilts of night
we murmured
as currents of the Yellow
River washed in sleep.
Such were our pleasures.
I did not know
that at dusk darkness
emerged from the human
mortar of the Great Wall
that all great rivers
had an undertow and
that trains could derail.
We now live
in separate cities.
It was in China
that the rift began.

Connie Johnstone

Hell's Kitchen

> *Now that God is news, what's left but prayer?*
> — Agha Shahid Ali

In the basement room under the bakery on 47th Street,
she sits in yeasty silence in a circle with her sangha.

Holding cradle pose, heads down and turned, they rock
starving Gaza babies, unsung lullabies rising.

Standing bent and leaning, searchlight pose, they sweep
flashlights, rescue Israelis, in tunnels, dark air stirring.

Eyes screen-burned from watching second-hand and
third-hand horror. Eardrums burst from words exploding.

They calm their minds in lotus pose. She climbs the stairs.
Swirls of baking scents are clinging, chasing her in the street.

Bread smells of its own small deaths, but she will be back
in the morning, to buy the bread, breathe it and break it, eat.

Anthony Xavier Jackson

Famine

What does death eat?
It eats images
Millions and millions
Of images.
Death gorges on
All your unwritten poems.
There goes Death
Sucking the breath
Of wandering golems.
A wayward
Fallen angel
Who grows fat
At the behest
Of the banquets
Left by faceless
Senseless
Drones

Death never eats alone
Death savors the cruelty
That consumes the downtrodden
Burping out a flagrant
Condemnation
Of anyone who does not
Look
Feel
Act
Pray
Sing
Like them.

How does death groom?

Death raises a razor
At my neck when
I genuflect for self
Respect in the corner
Of a dark booth
Where fingers pry holes
In walls

Begging for my essence
To spit
On the floor.

Where does death loom?

Death broods in a mist
Blankets all it touches
With insincerity
Placing a noncommittal kiss
On the lips
As it asks
Can you live with this?
It lisps
As it vomits chorine
All over your bliss.

How does death bloom?

Death sits on the shoulders
Of madmen with their
Fingers on the button
While brown babies
In Gaza are vaporized
Into vengeance's oblivion

Death tears down the hands
That would feed them
Feed them
Feed them
Feed…

But, what does death eat?

It eats the apple of your eye
The flavor of the crack of your ribs
The tearing of your ACL
All the machines we abandon in the sky
Death eats your granny's stories
When she forgets the names
And her eyes start to focus
She sits there worried
Of strange men in bushes
Naked priests in the trees

Death eats your beliefs

But can't stand the taste
Of faith

Faith takes its appetite
Right away.

Where does death wait?

In the center
Of your best intentions
Scraping your skull
Like a plate.

Nora Laila Goff

The Basil Can Save Us

Pray to the tomatoes and peppers
to take away our burdens.
Look not to the celestial sky
for your salvation look to the garden.
The basil grows two feet tall
in my garden in chill wind November.
I cut the basil top leaves for Romesco sauce.
First, I roast and peel sweet peppers from
the Sunday farmer's market.
Instead of church I walk
among the many Carmichael produce stands.
Back home in my garden
the lower leaves of the basil
Turn yellow from frosty nights.
Soon the basil stops growing
with brown stems and dying leaves.
It cannot save itself from the cycle of life
and enters the underworld
leaving hope in the form of seeds
smaller than faith.

Andy Jones

Babassu Fronds

I have a name for you.
It is spoken softly
as I bring you up some water.

My compass has settled
at true north,
and you are my magnet
I have ceased wandering.

Someone has watered the ferns.
Someone has sorted the darks.
Someone has packed a lunch.
Someone has remembered.

Someone has remembered
a patina of evaporation
that surrounds your soft cheeks,
a waterfall that roars distantly.

In this vaporous jungle,
a Babassu palm tilts its fronds,
itself reflecting my own admiration.

We do not have names
for the innumerable stars,
but I have a name for you.

Jane Rosenberg LaForge

Haunted Mansion

Of all the rare occasions
my father demonstrated
tenderness toward my mother
during their marriage, I remember
best the trip to Disneyland.
We had just finished our
tour of the Haunted Mansion,
with its uncanny apparitions,
grotesque yet anesthetized
to suppress their power
and significance; they danced
at a ball and hitched rides
with children, friendly
if disenchanted corpses
imbued with a neon
derivative; and our father
wanted to know if she was
all right, how she was coping,
with hallucinations she was
scolded for abashedly believing
just months earlier, now acceptable
to acknowledge and share with
the common people. She replied
she was diverting herself, speculating
on how Disneyland pulled this off,
whether by cameras or mirrors or
some heretofore secret technology
that could be put to more perilous
usage should it fall into the hands
of the Russians. My father was
relieved, as the red menace
had always been one of their
favorite topics, the threat from
a foreign source that had nothing
to do with them, their unapproachable
values and ethics; and everything to do
with their fear of failure; of being called
out for their fantasy lives as resolute
Americans and responsible parents.

Mary Mackey

Prophecy of the Trees

we are a sacred beast without a name
a single living body
ten billion white candles
topped with green flame
sucking water from the earth
speaking in a language you don't understand
wide as infinity
silent as the moment that comes
just after death

we toss your planes into the clouds
fill your nights with a million moving shadows
create our own weather

roots tangled
vines twisting around us
like a snake of stars
we are as unstoppable as rain

Listen   Here is our prophecy:

when the songs of the macaws
become ghost songs
and the frogs goes mute
and the cicadas stop humming
when nothing walks or talks
or wanders among us but you
and the only sound in the jungle
is the sound of your voices
we will become the great love you lost
the hope you abandoned
the fires that burn you
the ashes that fill your lungs

Melisa McCampbell

Pruners' Code

> Inspired by David Matsumoto's *Epitaph for a Peach*

Seeing with next year's eyes
I follow the branch to the end
And allow the image to rise

I conjure up shape and size
With unknown knot and bend
Seeing with next year's eyes

The small fruit yet to be realized,
The tight bud, the green leaf to tend
I allow the image to rise

I bring bee and bug and spring's bird cries
All in my mind of hopes and pretend
Seeing with next year's eyes

There, in my palm, nature's prize
Plucked from a limb still with shoots to send
And all the image to rise

While fragrance fills the air, even as it dies
I keep to the task at hand
Seeing with next year's eyes
I allow the image to rise

Moira Magneson

Two Weeks Into The New Administration

This morning I am a citizen
of the dark. Someone — *who?* —
has driven a car
into a telephone pole,
the whole grid gone out.
Not a light anywhere for miles.
Stunned, I stumble through
my house as if I had never lived
here before. I can no longer
negotiate the arrangement
of furniture — the sudden sharp
corners, everything larger
and hazardous in its black
shadow. Papers strewn
everywhere. Cats like little
sentries pacing the hall,
howling discontent. They know
something is wrong. Still,
with every room I enter
I flip switches, conditioned
for the cause/effect
of forthcoming light. I tell
myself *it cannot always be
night*, though I do not quite
believe it.

Half-Life

Blacksburg, Virginia — April 16, 2007

When loneliness enters the house
of the body, it knows where
to go — the heart's uneasy chair.
It slumps, sucks in atmosphere.
Dense as cobalt, it broods,
heavy shadow growing heavier
until the room goes entirely dark.
Windows sealed with foil. No light.
Years tick by. The house lives
at midnight. No moon. No stars.
Finally. It has a plan. All it takes
is a word, a look, a laugh. It hatches
its heat. Hollow at the core. Invisible.
Detached. It eases out the door
to do its work for the day —
to the college, catching two people
by surprise. To the post office
waiting in line behind taxpayers.
Smell of iron on its soles. It mails
a package. Undetected. A short drive
back to the science building. Chains
clanking. We can hear it now. Footfall
in the stairwell. Moving classroom to
classroom. Making its rounds. Unleashing
its half-life. Fury. Entering forty-seven
bodies. Putting the gun to its own.
The last thing it wants — understanding,
forgiveness. Above all else. Deep in
the limbic. It desires to go on.

Rita Fuhr Marowitz

Hard Lessons

Along a foggy path
bordered with silvery eucalyptus
and ragged purply wild iris
I come upon
the still warm
but headless
body of a hummingbird,
iridescent breast still quivering,
obscene now
without its whirring, winged soul.

Driving south on 280
I take pleasure in
the slow sexy curves of the smooth road,
the false mastery of changing
from lane
to lane
to lane,
the eternal swish of tires.
Vivaldi washes over me from four speakers.
Soon enough I will exit
and prepare to greet
whatever remains of my father
after six weeks on the cancer ward.

In a Chinese restaurant on Pacific
I chat with Kathy
over bowls of sizzling rice soup,
spooning up the news
of all the old crowd.
Fast-tracking
free-lancing,
postcards from Peru.
New houses, new babies
Ex-husbands, lost lovers.
We skillfully wield our chopsticks
consider where to have dessert
agree we've done as well,
at least as all the rest.

I have these questions —
about the cruelties of nature
about pain
about the failures of self.

I have these answers —
a hummingbird carcass
my father's face stretched tight and gray by pain
the mixed fates and early deaths of friends and lovers.
We love who we find.
We love how we can.

If you drive fast enough,
the line of lights rimming the bay
will blur
and obscure for a time
death's shadow
just one lane over.

Deborah Melvedt

Apology

I didn't say goodbye to my father or my boyfriend
of five years because I thought I would see them again.
The same with the first cat and the second.
But not the dog or my mother whose deaths
we controlled
co-signers with God
withdrawing needles or
sinking steel into the thinnest of skins.

With both of you
I said goodbye over and over
sitting bedside with Jesus
stroking grey fur
touching silver white hair
leaning in to whisper
I love you
I'm sorry
over and over and over again
like lullabies or the throw of a ball
for the hundredth time on a summer day.

When they ask you what you like about your body and all you can say is my collarbones

In humans, two of our 206 bones
are collarbones
sharp bridges between sternum and scapula
the grace men finger on women
who strut in strapless dresses
across a summer room.

In birds, they are called wishbones
tender marrow we snap on holidays
our fingers wrapped in wanting
the longest piece worth more
than grace said at the dinner table.

In sea mammals, the clavicle is absent
whales and dolphins have no place for
swaggering the world,
their leap so perfect
without vanity or prayer.

Ann Michaels

Daughters Dreaming in the Bones of an Absent Father

in medias res

not a breath of air, nor ripple on the water save
for the foam the oars made: men tired
from travel row an eager Odysseus bound
on a cross, find safe harbor at the western
edge of the world.

Sirena

underneath my skin, that place below
where melanin burns, darkens and lightens with time.
there, beyond the dermis where cells multiply: encoded
in memory, a secret breathes in silence
scratching the layer from the inside.
i whispered you once, believed: lungs that breathe salt water
can breathe air. i followed from the sea, you
on land, a spasm, drawn out in echoes.

i knew the rhythm.
eons of ebb and flow, white edges
where unfortunate souls, lost in despair
risked their flesh in search of the absent lover.
tongues cut to walk on land, legs bleed
with each and every step.

my body knew the secret, harbored it well.
the secret stung, burning my insides to hollow.
there were dusks my body bruised with longing,
and dawns, cut from waking. i could not
cry nor sing, could not see, i did not want to be seen.

lost into white foam and spray, the last gasp
i willingly gave. i could not catch
my breath, no sea water. i had no wish for forgetting.
i had no spell, nor incantation to conjure
the lover who did not come home.

island dreaming

awake. i wish i could count the stars at dawn as they fade
into morning, catch the shadow with my eye, the faint outline
of the moon before it disappears. then, i would not have to witness
the ruins here. on sand, old stones crumble where a foundation stood.
concrete walls, irresistible to weight and time
wrought weary and decayed. the sun lights cobblestones,
enters spaces through the roof, holes poked through
from the network of palm and raffia. at night,
rain wears basalt, subterranean eruptions burst pillows,
breaking.

Casey Mills

Home State

sensual hills, broken by fences
grass unperturbed, tree limbs weighted with water
coursing through veins in hard summer sun

how quickly this California country's
story took shape, conquer then divide
with rough-hewn fence posts, twisted wire

which then transformed, 10-acre ranchettes
white plastic fences, landscaped patchworks as
sheep and cattle melt into gleaming lake boats

clearly sacred yet sickly kept, despite all our
kind ideas, this state still enthralled with a plan:
break these sensual hills. break them with fences

In the End

generous notions
the water gathers
through storm drains
to starving creeks

water that feeds and kills
turning willows vibrating green
while raking vines downstream
plucked from streambed and flailing

beaver's home the greatest casualty
she raises her tail in anger
at these dam-destroying storms
that pay her and her palace no mind

this is our winter now
generous notions, gathering water
to cleanse us by the very joy
that in the end may carry us away

MLuv

The Process

In the winds of mental detail, I open the ear of my heart and hear the pleasing sounds of the space I occupy.

In the silences, the vast in between of it all lies communication.

Free information for the tuned in. The receivers.

Intuition screams. Body receives. Trigger points lead the reaction.

Skin surface ripples. Nerves send signals. Noses pick up the scent in skin.

A gnawing knowing leads a flow all of its own.

Connection assured like gum on sidewalks attach to rubber soles in the height of Sacramento summer heat.

I'm hopelessly stuck.

Caught up in golden threads dangling from my headspace tying up thought processes in dizzying mental gymnastics.

Gale force winds whip thoughts around like dry dead leaves play when they think no one is looking.

Life is a date with the willing and unwilling.

Ebony Patiño

I am a Whoaman

With many limitations I still keep faith
I go and compete
While wearing beat face
Always number 1 so yes, I will stay in my place
Lose fuel every month but still keep up the pace
Get everything done without leaving a trace
No bragging or boasting or credit to claim
Can be carrying two and expected to do the same
Embrace the changes and stay in my lane
Control my emotions so I'm not viewed as insane
Exceed expectations while still looking pretty
Need nobody's help sympathy no pity
Carry the strength of Samson with so much more to bear
Give birth to humanity and flip back my hair
Though I appreciate man, you are not
My identity
Anything you can do I can do,
Identically…

Jennifer O'Neill Pickering

First Star on the First Night of the New Year

There is silence this pandemic spawned
that made me feel like I was in church.
I *was* a soloist in a Methodist choir.
This nightingale's voice is dearer.

Coyote's howl reminds me
my cat's domesticity
won't stop her roaming nights.
She can't be tamed nor can I.

I make a Pagan wish
on the brightest star, Sirius
to carry a message on swift legs
for peace, a kinder year.

I am not Christian except when
I need a favor,
close my eyes, bow my head,
pray to stop smoking,
whisper a compline for strength,
to escape the devil
parading as a husband,
a daughter's happiness,
a second husband to heal.

I've always made these deals
with the Christian God
with a promise in return
of being a better person.

The star glints from
the middle branch of the Tulip tree
burgeoning buds the color of fawns
vow of blushing bells to ring in spring.

My father got God in his last years
touched by the light, surrendered
to a higher power, went
from EST, AA, to Jesus.

I am the sacrist to this tree,
she the priestess marking seasons,
worshipping the stars and moon.
Death around the corner,
birth on its shoulders.

Shawn Pittard

Thin Places

There were whitecaps on the water.
The wind riffled in your hair

as you watched
the river fill my waders
its current take me —

watched me
swim for the safety of an eddy
where I clawed and crawled my way out.

You sat next to me on the coarse gravel.
That was a close call, you said.

Like that slip on the icefield on Grand Teton.
Or that bluff charge by a bull sea lion in the Sea of Cortez.

*How about those bastards
at that Desert Center truck stop
that tried to get the drop on you?*

Your voice was a defiant scoff.

We made it, you said,
All the way to here.

Cottonwood down swirled around us.
I studied you.

You asked,
Am I how you've imagined?

Danyen Powell

Lake Tahoe at Noon

turquoise brooch
pinned
to the forest floor

piers wade
into a timelessness

granite boulders
float
on the surface tension

       *

broken clouds stall
enchanted
by their own reflection

    a ring of mountains
doubles the size of this dream

       *

unblocked sun   blue rifts
snowflakes fall
         out of clear sky

wind breaks from the summit
down through the pines
whistling its one note

Ross Powers

Unhoused

The roof has flown away
fragile contents of me exposed
wind-whipped pages of books
the direct glare of sunlight
everywhere in my rooms

One ordinary incident did it
a single death (a friend, a wife)
among thousands who die each day
stripped me naked to the sky
a shocked creature without its rock

Tented on the street, living from a car?
there must be more, something more
to my time left above the earth
arms outstretched to touch it
old, blunted antenna twitching

A garden is wanted, a compost pile
some seasons, four is enough
to grow worms, carrots, a bag of spuds
no roof to stop the rain from falling
or block the heat of our brilliant star

Rick Rayburn

The Fresno Poet

> *Long nights & absent dawns & a little mercy in the tea*
> — from Phillip Levine's *The Second Going*

Niñas y niños dribble a rubber ball along
the oil-sprayed dirt alley. Restless nights
prey on the grape cutters — blisters, tedium &
hopelessness from wooden handled pruners. Never absent,
the Mexicans at red dawn's
awakening, lineup on the vineyard's raisin trays &
tomorrow's promise. The gritty poet, wearing a
Motor City t-shirt, witnesses from across the little
canal where they kneel washing their faces. Mercy
neglects a mother pausing to nurse in
between furrows lined with gray chokeweed. The
farm laborers far from accordions and Jesuit's tea.

Sandra Rendig

Hour Of Dancing Wings

Driving at dusk on a country road
In the Sacramento Valley,
windows down,
breathing cool, sweet earth,
the moist scent of plant and soil.

Without the blinding heat of day
my vision is renewed —
rows of sunflowers, tall and leafy
every yellow head bowing to the setting sun.

The broad, smooth river meanders
through the land of rice, tomatoes, corn.
Long rows of almond trees flash by
and shrink into the distance.

This is the hour of dancing wings —
delicate mayflies, white moths, darting bats
and black crows heading home.

The sky unearths me
with swaths of blazing colors —
rose, peach, apricot and a golden
glow over the dark mountains
where the fiery dragon
has just slipped
out of sight.

Sweet Grief

The last days of fall are full
of hazy, honey light and
crisp, cool breath.
The trees release
their restless leaves
to fly, to die, to decompose,
ultimately a chance
to live again.

I, too, feel this sweet
grief of autumn
when the sun is quiet,
nights are chilly-dark,
and the bold, full moon
glows icy cold.

I feel it in my bones
and see it in the mirror:
my body weathered,
veined, wrinkled —

my story from the first
bloom of spring
to the last sigh of autumn,
revolving toward
the inevitable
final season.

Melinda Rivasplata

All The Colors You Can Feel

Light purple Sierra asters, dark blue and purple lupines
Paint brush of all sizes reds, magenta-pinks
Color popping red, purple blue, blue blue, purple
Mountain pennyroyal, horse mint
Pollinators sphinx moth extending proboscis
Solitary bees black fuzzy with yellow stripes
Pollen packed, busy busy busy flying
Flitting over wildflower dense sideways meadows
Falling from the slopes of Elephant Back
Mules ears' soft pettable leaves
Sun breeze color huff and puff up the trail
Large ants under foot, grasshoppers flashing yellow wings
Clark's nutcrackers raucous in the white bark
Pines with clustered needle bundles
White pine, lodgepole Hemlock nodding
White blanched trees collapsed branches
Pointing at the sky gray granite underfoot
Winnemucca Lake blue as full as I have seen it
Shrinking snow fields on Round Top's slopes

Allegra Silberstein

A gravel road

winds its way
    into morning
        sun streams
            golden
  it's light
  mirrored in
left-over pools
    from
    last night's rain
        and fences
  delineate fields
      brown stubble
    where
        I have died

narrow road
   continues
     rising up
       under shadows
     of bare trees
   there are no
signs
    telling me
       where to go
    unseen
  in morning
      stillness
this blue sky
  of separation

Yuriy Serebriansky

Ашаршылық

> Казахский голод 1930–1933

Каждой весной, примерно в это же самое время
привозная генетическая память моего деда
заставляла всю нашу семью сажать картошку.
Если вы думаете, что в СССР плохо было с картошкой,
нет, это было лучшее время!
По осени мы выкапывали те же четыре мешка
совершенно другой картошки
половина гнила зимой.
Дед так и не понял другого способа жить
на этой земле без корней
брал в руки баян и играл застольные
и сырые голоса старух отпевали
картошку в погребе под нашими ногами.

Asharshylyq

Kazakh Famine 1932-1933

Each spring my family plant potatoes
every year like clockwork
guided by my grandpa's genetic memory brought from afar.
And if you think the USSR lacked potatoes
no, we had plenty, more than ever.
Then in the autumn we would dig up the same four bags
of completely different potatoes
and half would rot in winter.
Grandpa never figured out another way to live
on this land with no roots.
He would take an accordion
play drinking songs
and raw voices of old women
became a requiem for the potatoes in the basement
under our feet.

(Translated by Ariadna Linn.)

Don Solomon

Climbing Butcher Hill

I do not belong here this early.
The sun just a hint in the eastern sky.
I cross the wooden bridge across the creek,
surprise two black-tailed does towing fawns.
Startled by my trespass, they glare indignantly,
flick their tails and melt into the brush.

I do not belong here, but neither do they,
less than 60 yards from an eight-lane freeway.
Tired truckers and early commuters
snake through the thin morning light.
I trespass in this little patch of oak forest,
stroll where grizzlies once ruled.
Now even the oaks and buckeyes must budge,
wild plums squeeze between their trunks,
toyons shoved aside by the
olive trees intruding on the hillside.

As I climb Butcher Hill, a tattle-tale scrub jay
warns of my approach, crying wolf,
rustling its blue feathers in a small oak.
Close to the end of my climb,
each step becomes a matter of will.
I crest the hill and look to the west.

A fine mist of fog clings lightly
to the hills of the coastal mountains.
Soft breeze threatening the heat to come.
My hands also cling to this land,
try to hold onto these few acres
of rolling hills, oaks, and buckeyes,
as the bulldozers and road graders
plant houses in the valley below.

Insomnia 3:04 a.m.

the stars are stupid   they
          will not   close their eyes
their blank stare   follows me

the moon's cold   fluorescence
          hums in my ears   pleading
for death   tired of resurrection

the pull   of the stars
          moon swaying   i should
forgive their trespass
          forgiveness is not   in me

wrapped in the night's tentacles
          if i surrender   i drown
in salty waves   of sleep

Bob Stanley

Where It Needs to Be

I'm reading your poem now, Rick,
The one you sent me to look at
So I might make a few suggestions
Before it goes into your book,
And I'm thinking it's close,
Really close. You're telling us
About the very first time you saw
Marianne, when she peeked into your Westwood fraternity room
At the sound of a song from a scratchy long-playing record
Behind your half-open door in 1965,
And you singing along like a corny lonesome cowboy
Which started everything.

I'm thinking, the poem's pretty much
Where it needs to be, you describe
Her clearly in stanza two
Shoulder length brunette
And then again in stanza four when she
Sneaks a waist-high wave to you from the dance floor
Where she's dancing with another guy.

I'm just about to tell you this —
Add a little more to fill the scene out
To bring her back into the focus at the end
In stanza six when you're buying her ice cream,
When I realize that right now, in real time
You've just taken her to the hospital
You and Marianne, who still recognizes you after
Fifty years together and nearly ten years more
Through her slow haze of forgetting
And you're sitting with her in the ER right now
Not sure how long she will
Go on, but you're there for her every day.

And being roused from the critique of a poem
Back to the real world where the two of you
Wait together for one more song, even if it is a distant one,
I pause before I hit Send, before
I might presume to edit even the smallest line of
Your perfect lives together, Rick and Marianne.
It's pretty much exactly where it needs to be.

Jeanine Stevens

Tule Elk

Cervus canadensis nannodes

A grand animal once widespread
along coast and valley.
Slow moving, tawny hide, elegant stride,
they favor sweet grass near Tomales Bay.

Tourists get close for a photo op.
Here a man pulls an aging Dachshund
along by its leash, ties him to a tripod.

A sign: "Observe from a distance,
raise your thumb, close one eye —
you may be too close"

I remember in college, we studied the eco-niche,
the degree of open space needed for survival.

Elk numbers dwindle, old game trails
fenced off, too high to hurdle.
Narrow confinement, dietary deficiency?

On my way home, I pick up a Glacéau,
"Smart water," check the photos in my phone:
only fog, barricades shrouded in fog.

I noticed where the elk nibbled —
they left a clump,
a carved bouquet of green.

Alex Stolis

Into the Land

> *But of the tree of the knowledge of*
> *good and evil, thou shalt not eat of it: for in the day*
> *that thou eatest thereof thou shalt surely die.*
> — Genesis 2:17

She knows, sometimes I practice dying;
fully-winged, eyes closed, waiting
for a crash of wind.

Someone passes the basket,
take what you need, leave the rest.
We get ready to preamble,

I catch her glance, imagine
we're lolling on a beach
in Kerouac's Mexico.

We're already there,
whiskeys in a row,
a tapestry of sand

and every prayer ever stuttered
is waiting for high tide
to wash us away.

Gary Thomas

Sunshine on the Giant Orange

No, nothing rhymes with it, and so
what? Nothing quite rhymes with
my recollection of Giant Orange
stands along US 99 in the Fifties,
either, when we spotted the bright
globoid building, pulled over, piled
out, got in line, already smelling
the wave of fresh citrus being *squoze* —
my favorite word at the age of eight —
and driveled at the sight of beaker-sized
tumblers being filled with pulpy elixir
the color of the Golden Gate Bridge
at sunrise. My mother and I slurped
ours as soon as they were handed
to us from the Orange's shadowy maw,
grinning at each other's overspill while
my father considered another item
on the placarded menu: Cold Keg
Beer to go with *Alaska-Sized* burgers.
In the end, though, he respected
his wife's membership in the local Women's
Christian Temperance Union, opted for
a small orange juice and *Texas-Sized* Fries.
We were all sticky, neon-orange-stained
and sated when we clambered back into
our '51 Dodge as sun's last sweet glint
struck the Orange. This morning I stuff
whole segments of a supermarket Valencia
down my gullet and try to believe this
rhymes with that ancient ride home.

Ziaeddin Torabi

Hanging Gardens

How much does this city look like a city
I had made in my childhood dreams.
A colossal and charming city

with towering and beauteous buildings
with spectacular alleys and streets
with big and small stores

crowded and noisy
with tall and lush trees
on both sides of its streets.

And the streams full of water
that always flowed
pleasantly singing

all around the city.
A city with large and small gardens around it
with trees full of colorful fruits

especially a majestic tree with red apples hanging
which tempted everyone to pick and eat them.
A charming and dreamy city

with winding alleys and streets
with stratified gardens
full of trees and lush

much like the legendary
hanging gardens
of Ancient Babylon.

Ann Wehrman

January in Sacramento

gray sky lowers
bare black branches
create calligraphic flourishes
rain falls for a week
gullies tip, creeks wash out low roads
river town takes long deep breaths
air perfumed by fecund earth
soaked tree bark

The Blue Hour

soft as a lambswool boa
fuchsia clouds stream across blue sky
that darkens each moment
vision soars upward
within deep azure expanse
too early for stars
looking down, black trees
pine or deciduous
hide their identities
as night expands

Patricia Wentzel

The Beckoning Bed

Rucked-up sheets,
slanting light of late afternoon,
two voices raised in laughter from the shower,
peonies in a crystal vase,
cat perched up high —
told the tale to even the untrained eye.

It had been a long time coming,
companionship the opening dance —
laboring at the side of the dying
their common ground,
their resistance to dark humor
marking them as different,
resilient, feet planted in the earth —
one a redwood, tall, sturdy,
the other a dogwood, gracious,
always reaching for the light.

The wine of discovery —
of shared passions —
puzzles, poetry, pastry
made at home from apricots
and ginger or plums from the tree
in the wilderness of an abandoned cottage garden —
left them tipsy like Sunday morning mimosas
made with fresh orange juice.

The passion of the body snuck up on them,
ambushed them under the plum tree —
the reaching arms crossing, fingers plucking
the small ripe fruit, the taller woman's
curly red hair tangling in the stunted twigs,
their breath mingling
when the other, gray-haired,
crow's feet and laugh lines plain,
drew the branch down, released
the auburn locks, one strand at a time.

They stood there together
while the hermit thrush sang in the
distance, the silence of the grove broken
by their quickened breaths,
mid-day light
illuminating the shared glance,
flush of longing,
newly born, tinting their cheeks.

Hesitant at first, then eager,
desire propelled them forward
hand-in-hand into wonder, delight,
across the garden, into the house,
then to the bedroom
and the beckoning bed,
the air sweetly scented,
cat crouched on the highboy chest,
blousy peonies in the vase.

Wendy Williams

Where Hawks Fly

Where hawks fly
follow each other treetop to treetop
and the red of Indian paintbrush
        surprises
as I rise up the hill following
        deer tracks
behind properties and trailers
        and trucks
up where the ridge rock towers
and spring flowers sprinkle
        the soft, crumbly dirt
where one could get hurt on barbed wire
        or wolf traps
if not careful. Up ahead the creamy butts
        of five black-tailed deer
so I steer toward the lower trails
and catch the dirt road to the power line
back from cedars and ponderosa pines
        back to civilization's line
away from surprise and the cry of hawks
one to another and maybe to me
lone traveler among the ridge slopes,
        among the piles of rotted, rusted cans
and great rocks left by volcano flow or glaciers
        way long ago
There I found my adventure today as the snow
        flakes fall faster
        my steps head home

Early Mornings

I am watching
for the hare to come bounding down the hill,
waiting for that peek of robin-orange
    to appear through the juniper branches
        just over the nest

waiting for the soft, gray doves
to alight on top of the telephone pole

for the magpies to start chattering
    their black and white

waiting for the cries of all the children of Gaza to quiet

    which will take lifetimes

meanwhile swamp water
    invites white herons to fish
smoky-gray storm clouds
    gather over the ridge
rain soaks the garlic, the chives,
    spearmint and thyme
and we all awake
    according to each of our world's rhyme

I am waiting for clouds to drift down
    from blue skies
and gift us with droplets of moisture

waiting for relief
of the hollow, hungry eyes of the children

Nanci Woody

A Sweeter Gift

What gift have I
to mark this day
one of countless days we have shared
days turned to years
years falling
tumbling rapidly into decades.

What gift have I
to mark this day
one of many such days
heartbreaking, some
most filled with joy.
We shared them all.

This day, by your bedside,
your hand in mine
I read to you
those favorite poems
we've shared in happier times.

Housman's emotional lines
early though the laurel grows
it withers quicker than the rose
and dear Emily's
hope is the thing with feathers.

Perhaps this day
I'll end our time together with Milton
who tried to
justify the ways of God to man
though justify I can not
this suffering wrought upon you.

What gift have I?
Only the gift of time
though nothing new
seems sweeter now
when days are few.

Andrena Zawinski

When I was just a kid

> *Do what you are going to do,
> and I will tell about it.*
> — Sharon Olds

I remember when I was just a kid, I was a runner
for my parents' daily numbers penciled onto
folded slips of white paper I handed
on tiptoes to the butcher bookmaker.

Afterwards, I'd pay for their Camels and Kools
with quarters fed to a vending machine at the door
that delivered shiny penny change inside clear
and crinkly cellophane wrappers I'd tear into

to buy strips of chocolate licorice twists
and the honey sweet crisp of Butterfingers
for the hike along the sidewalk home.

And when my father's vodka crossed the table,
I turned escape artist adventurist off to nearby
woods wandering hours under cool shade
and dappled sun until streetlights came on.

I even devised a disappearing act behind a bureau
and vanity, under a desk and bed, when the leather
strap slid through its loops, raw rice mat on the floor.

Now I rub the dimples of long scarred knees
and remember, wince at the welt of belt across thighs,
and remember, sprawl beneath the shelter of pines,
dark Doves in the pocket, and remember.

Stan Zumbiel

The Sea Calls Me Back

I don't listen and head for tree-covered mountains just across a two-lane road ignoring speeding cars and the sea's whispered attempts at seduction. A man sits in a lighthouse and studies infinite combinations of night waves. I imagined ten years ago that was the way to spend my life, that the quiet would lead to brilliant thoughts, that dreams would become crisp and clear in the repetitive breaking of water. You can't build your life on light even as it reaches through the dark – a warning. I move away, and trees block the view of the sea. With each increase in elevation, silence transforms, becomes air mixed with trees. Each shadow moves, alive with wind and sunlight. Blackbirds, sparrows, and the unseen meadowlark mark my path with song.

Bird First for Joy

Comes the opening of light! The first bird
frees its throat, splits the window, and before
breakfast breathes an early prayer.

Begin the morning with sunlight and Bach,
rooms swollen with music, garden clear
and full with the outside world — birds
entering the birdbath, needle-thin water
creating a rainbow, a spray of divided
color the ancients saw in waterfalls.

Windows project morning, dreams
on both sides, the side seen waking
and the side shown only to those asleep.

Look at what can be done with a cello.
Stay away from that dark void.

Await a future free of words from cloudy
mountains where trees imagine black
shadows cursed to outlive all except the sea.

Tule 87 Review

ABOUT THE CONTRIBUTORS

Matthew J. Andrews, a Californian now living in Iowa, is a private investigator and writer. He is the author of the chapbook *I Close My Eyes and I Almost Remember* and the forthcoming full-length collection *The Hours* (Solum Press). He can be contacted at www.matthewjandrews.com.

Paul Aponte is a Chicano Poet from Sacramento. He is a member of the writers group Escritores Del Nuevo Sol, and also a board member of Círculo De Poetas & Writers. He has been published in several anthologies, the latest being in *Voices 2024*, and has a new book out called *DEL CACTUS* available through Prickly Pear Press and Amazon.com.

Catherine Arra is a native of the Hudson Valley in upstate New York, where she lives with wildlife and changing seasons until winter, when she migrates to the Space Coast of Florida. She is the author of eight poetry collections. Arra teaches part-time and facilitates local writing groups. Find her at www.catherinearra.com.

John Bell earned an MFA in creative writing from Wichita State University and retired from American River College. His poetry has appeared in *Thorny Locust*, *Sacramento Voices*, *Burning the Little Candle*, and elsewhere.

Lynn Belzer, a San Francisco native, began her path to poetry in 2016 after losing her husband. Now retired from her psychotherapy-organizational coaching career, Belzer's work weaves inner and outer life, drawing on nature, art, daily events, and humor. She is active in Sacramento's poetry scene and has studied with Ellen Bass, Susan Kelly-DeWitt, Gillian Conolly, and Dorianne Laux.

Catherine Bridge is a retired journalist/adjunct English professor who has taught writing at Sacramento City and Sierra Colleges locally, and at colleges in Sonoma County as well as at Syracuse University and in Penang, Malaysia. She has been a reporter in New York City, and for the Sacramento Bee's Neighbors and Capitol Alert as well as for the San Francisco Recorder. Her poems have appeared in local anthologies, and she had recently completed a memoir.

Katy Brown is a poet and photographer. She has won awards in The Ina Coolbrith Circle, California Federation of Chaparral Poets, and The International Dance Poetry competition. Her poetry has appeared in numerous journals: *Sutterville Review*, *Song of San Joaquin*, *Poetalk*, *Persimmon Tree*, *Harpstrings*, and others. And anthologies: *Poeming Pigeons*, *Sacramento Voices*, *California Fire and Water*, and The Ina Coolbrith Society's *Gathering*. With Taylor Graham, she lead a quarterly "Capturing Wakamatsu" event featuring poetry and exploration of the historic American River Conservancy site.

From his home, **John Allen Cann** slips the half-mile down Sunset Drive to Anchor Bay beach almost daily: here he reads, writes, & enjoys the myriad moods of the seashore, often in sustained reverie. Chamber music & baseball continue to nourish him. He's always happy to return home after sundown to see the lights on in the Art Box Studio, where his wife, Robyn, is engaging her art. His most recent book is a lovely collaboration of his poetry & the art of painter, Mike Conner, *Thresholds*. Another collaboration with Connor, *Brevities*, is in the works for July 2025.

Sharon Coleman is a fifth-generation Northern Californian with a penchant for languages and their entangled word roots. She co-curates the reading series Lyrics & Dirges and co-directs the Berkeley Poetry Festival. She's the author of a chapbook of poetry, *Half Circle* and a book of micro-fiction, *Paris Blinks*. Her work appears *in Your Impossible Voice*, *White Stag*, and *Berkeley Poetry Review*. She received the Maverick Award for her poetry from the ruth weiss Foundation and the eco-poetry award for haiku from the Filoli Foundation. She teaches poetry and creative writing at Berkeley City College. See her website: Sharoncolemanpoetry.com.

Sue Daly's poetry has been featured in several literary journals and anthologies. Her chapbook, *A Voice at Last*, was published in 2017 by Dad's Desk Publishing Co. In 2021, Cold River Press published her poetry collection, *Language of the Tea Leaves*. Sue has facilitated poetry writing groups in Sacramento, CA for several years. She is enjoying retirement after working as a County of Sacramento Administrative Services Officer. For more information about her books and readings, e-mail Sue at jtwnana7@gmail.com.

Lucille Lang Day is the author of seven full-length poetry collections and four chapbooks. Her latest collection is *Birds of San Pancho and Other Poems of Place* (Blue Light, 2020). She has also edited the anthology *Poetry and Science: Writing Our Way to Discovery*, coedited *Fire and Rain: Ecopoetry of California* and *Red Indian Road West: Native American Poetry from California*, and published two children's books and a memoir, *Married at Fourteen: A True Story*. Her many honors include the Blue Light Poetry Prize, two PEN Oakland – Josephine Miles Literary Awards, the Joseph Henry Jackson Award, and eleven Pushcart Prize nominations. The founder and publisher of a small press, Scarlet Tanager Books, she lives in Oakland, California. https://lucillelangday.com

Karen DeFoe's poetry has appeared in *Voices of Lincoln Poetry Contest Winners Chapbook* (2019-2022); *Ink Spots: Award-winning Flash Fiction and Poetry, Gold Country Writers 10th Anniversary Anthology* (2022); *More Than Enough, An Anthology from The Sacramento Poetry Center Writing Groups* (2023); and *Tule Review* (2023).

Tino De Guevara has worked from a commercial salmon fisherman in Alaska's Bristol Bay to the culturally diverse streets of Fresno where he served as a dispute resolution mediator. In addition, he taught English classes in the jails and was a "Road Warrior" adjunct instructor at several California Community Colleges in the Bay Area. Tino walked the Camino de Santiago, a pilgrimage from France to Galicia, Spain, on a 500-mile journey in 2018. He and his wife, Maria-Elena, plan to walk through Greece in 2025. Currently, he lives in Fresno where he teaches English at Clovis Community College

Cindy Domasky lives in Sacramento, CA and found the wonderful Sacramento writing community many years ago; Sacramento Poetry Center (SPC), Amherst Writers and Artists (AWA), and volunteering with 916 INK and Read On, enjoying every minute. She has been published in *916 Ink, Saltwater*, and *Soul of the Narrator*.

Bob Eakins is currently a mostly retired senior citizen living in Sacramento, California. When he works, he is an adjunct faculty member at Sacramento City College.

Born in New York City, **Mary Eichbauer** makes her home in Benicia, California. Her first book of poetry, *After the Opera*, was published by Random Lane Press in 2020. Other publications include a book of literary criticism entitled *Poetry's Self-Portrait: The Visual Arts as Mirror and Muse in René Char and John Ashbery* (1992) and a collaborative poetry anthology called *Love's Meditation*, with Johanna Ely, Laurie Hailey, and Deborah Bachels Schmidt. Her poems have been recognized with awards from the Poets' Dinner and the Ina Coolbrith Circle Poetry Contest. She currently serves as Editor-in-Chief of Benicia Literary Arts

Susan Flynn is a poet, photographer, and psychologist living in Sacramento and Georgetown, California. Her first poetry collection, *Seeing Begins in the Dark*, was published by River Rock Books of Sacramento in June 2022. Susan is trained in the Amherst Writers and Artist's method and facilitates writing groups in local non-profits using the AWA method.

Laura Garfinkel is a certified Amherst Writers & Artists facilitator. She retired from a career as a medical social worker. Her poems have appeared or are forthcoming in *Feral: A Journal of Poetry & Art*, *Moss Piglet*, *Tule Review*, *Last Stanza*, and elsewhere. On weekends, she loves to hike with her family.

Callie Goff is a writer and adjunct professor from the Sierra Nevada Foothills.

Nora Laila Goff's chapbook of poetry is called The River Speaks. She co-hosted a poetry reading called Poemspirits for five years. She is a watercolor artist who paints local landscapes and flowers.

Tom Goff is an instructional assistant in the Reading and Writing Center at Folsom Lake College. He's written five poetry chapbooks. His first full-length poetry collection, *Twelve-Tone Row: Music in Words*, was published in 2018 (I Street Press). Tom won the Robinson Jeffers Tor House Prize for Poetry, 2021. His poems have been published in *Suisun Valley Review*, FLC's *The Parlay*, *Spectral Realms* (Hippocampus Press, NY), *Fire and Rain: Ecopoetry of California* (Scarlet Tanager Press), the 2023 and 2024 editions of *Voices* (Cold River Press), *Tule Review*, and *Medusa's Kitchen*.

Dr. Jeremy DeWayne Greene (aka G~Mile) is a nationally certified school psychologist as well as a poet/hip-hop artist. Although residing within the Sacramento region, his familial roots remain firmly planted in Baton Rouge, Louisiana. In his free time, Dr. Greene enjoys gathering and sharing the stories that he has heard along those winding roads...stories that include his time living and working as a school psychologist in Shanghai, China from 2017-2019.

Anara Guard is author of the prize-winning novel, *Like a Complete Unknown*, a collection of short stories, and two poetry collections: *Kansas, Reimagined* and *Hand on My Heart*. Her poems have been nominated for a Pushcart Prize and have received the John Crowe Ransom Poetry Prize from Kenyon College, a Jack Kerouac prize, and first place from the California State Poetry Society. Her writing has been published in *Persimmon Tree*, *On the Seawall*, *Gold Man Review*, *Under the Gum Tree*, a *New York Times* Tiny Love Story, and elsewhere. www.anaraguard.com

Jan Haag taught writing as a journalism/creative writing professor in Sacramento for more than three decades. Now retired, she hosts writing workshops using the Amherst Writers & Artists method and trains facilitators in the method. She is editor of AWA Press as well as the author of a poetry collection, *Companion Spirit*, and she has had stories and poems published in many anthologies and literary journals. She writes and posts daily poems on her website, janishaag.com.

Jocelyn Heath is an Associate Professor in English at Norfolk State University. Her first poetry collection, *In the Cosmic Fugue*, came out in November 2022 from Kelsay Books. Other creative writing has also appeared in T*he Atlantic, Crab Orchard Review, Poet Lore, Sinister Wisdom, Flyway,*and *Fourth River*. Her book reviews have appeared at *Lambda Literary, Entropy, The Lit Pub,*and elsewhere. She is an Assistant Editor for *Smartish Pace*.

Dianna Henning taught through California Poets in the Schools, received several California Arts Council grants and taught poetry workshops through the William James Association's Prison Arts Program, including Folsom Prison, and she runs The Thompson Peak Writers' Workshop from 1994 to present. Her publications include *The Power of the Feminine*, 2024; Blue Heron Review 2024; *The Tule Review*; 2024 *Verse Virtual 2024; Mocking Heart Review*, 2024; *Poet News*, Sacramento 2024; and *Artemis Journal*, among many others. She holds an MFA in Writing from Vermont College and has multiple Pushcart nominations.

Sibilla Hershey was born in Riga, Latvia and came to the US at the age of 15 as a World War II displaced person. Hershey taught at Solano Community College and worked for the State of California. She has published poems in *Rattlesnake Review, Yolo Crow, Entering, Tule Review, Voices 2023*, and in several anthologies. Hershey is also the author of a memoir entitled, *The Girl from Riga*, which describes her experiences of growing up in a war zone, life in refugee camps, adjustment to life in the United States, and subsequent search for happiness.

David Holper has done a little bit of everything: taxi driver, fisherman, dishwasher, bus driver, soldier, house painter, bike mechanic, bike courier, and teacher. He has three collections of poetry: *Language Lesson: A Linguistic Hejira* (Deeper Magic Press, 2023), *The Bridge* (Sequoia Song Publications) *and 64 Questions* (March Street Press). His poems have appeared in numerous literary journals and anthologies. He is an emeritus professor at College of the Redwoods and lives in Eureka, California, where he is the city's first Poet Laureate. He thinks Eureka is far enough from the madness of civilization that he can still see the stars at night and hear the Canada geese calling.

Anthony Xavier Jackson is a poet and musician whose work may be found on SoundCloud and Bandcamp. Jackson has been writing since his teenaged years. From the Last Poets to Nikki Giovanni, from Punk Rock to Crossroads Blues, he is a proud inheritor of the traditions of Afropunk, Afrosurrealism, Afrofuturism — all wrapped up in a 21st century American experience. He is a founding member of the Sacramento poetry collective GTFO. He has recently been published in such journals as *Wingless Dreamer, Bar Bar, The Word's Faire*, and *new words press*.

Poetry writing found **Connie Johnstone** in 2021; her poems have appeared or are forthcoming in *The Scarred Tree: Poetry of Moral Injury; Ravenous: le terroir du Montolieu; The Amethyst Review* and many others. She also published a novel, *The Legend of Olivia Cosmos Montevideo* (Atlantic Monthly Press); edited an anthology, *I've Always Meant to Tell You* (Pocket Books); was a professor of English and chair of creative writing at American River College; changed careers and was a hospice chaplain with Kaiser Permanente. She earned an MFA from Bennington and an MTS from Harvard Divinity School. She lives and writes in Davis, California.

Dr. Andy Jones is a writing professor, radio talk show host, journalist, and the poet laureate *emeritus* of Davis, California. He has taught writing, creative writing and literature classes at the University of California, Davis since 1990, and during those years has hosted over 2,000 events. Dr. Andy has published essays on Lord Byron, John Keats, T.S. Eliot, Elizabeth Bishop, Robert Lowell, and Amiri Baraka. His books of poetry include *Split Stock, Where's Jukie?,* In the Almond Orchard: Coming Home from War*, and, last year, a book of 100 poems that he wrote for his wife.

Jane Rosenberg LaForge is the author of four full-length collections of poetry; four chapbooks of poetry; a memoir; and two novels. Her fifth full-length collection will be *The Exhaust of Dreams Adulterated* from Broadstone Books in 2025. More poetry has been published or is forthcoming in *Poetry South, Cottonwood, Freshwater Literary Journal, Pictura Journal,* and *Twelve Mile Review.*

Mary Mackey is the author of *The Jaguars That Prowl Our Dreams: New and Selected Poems 1974 to 2018,* Winner of the 2019 Eric Hoffer Award for the Best Book Published by a Small Press, and a CIIS Women's Spirituality Book Award; and *The Village of Bones: Sabalah's Tale,* a novel about Prehistoric Europe; plus 7 other collections of poetry and 13 other novels. Her latest book, *Creativity: Where Poems Begin* is a nonfiction look at the origins of inspiration. Join her mailing list at http://eepurl.com/CrLHT and find more information at https://marymackey.com/

Moira Magneson's full-length collection of poems *In the Eye of the Elephant* will be published by Sixteen Rivers Press in 2025. Her novella, *A River Called Home—a river fable,* illustrated by Robin Center, was released by Toad Road Press in early 2024. Currently, she is the poet-in-residence for ForestSong, a traveling art project exploring solastalgia, biophilia, and resilience in the face of wildfire devastation.

Originally from the Bay Area, **Rita Fuhr Marowitz** retired a while ago after having been an English teacher, a writer/editor, a marketing manager and a staff services manager with California's Medi-Cal program. She is passionate about her husband, travel, reading, museums, quilting, chocolate, and always adopting rescue dogs. Her life mantra: be kind and be courageous!

Melisa McCampbell writes to understand the world and her place in it. By sharing her thoughts and words, she hopes to ignite that spark of recognition and connect with others in the petri dish of life. She works as a speech therapist and lives with her best friend, Benji, the dog. They both enjoy long walks in the green belt next to their home.

Deborah Meltvedt is a public health educator and writer in Sacramento, California. She has been published in various literary anthologies including *Intima: A Journal of Narrative Medicine,*
the Creative Non-Fiction Anthology *What I Didn't Know: True Stories of Becoming a Teacher.* Her first book of poetry *Becoming a Woman* was published in 2022. Deborah lives with her husband, Rick, and their cat, Anchovy Jack.

Ann Michaels was born in the Philippines and lives in California. She teaches English at UC Davis and CSU, Sacramento, and has also directed CSU's University Reading & Writing Center. A writer of poetry and prose, her work explores intersections between family, identity, and migration. Ann, who has sung vocal jazz at both Sacramento State and American River College, has served on the board of the Sacramento Poetry Center and is a regular host at Twin Lotus Thai's Fourth Tuesday Poetry Series. Ann is currently working on a hybrid novel entitled *Growin' Up California*.

Casey Mills writes poems early in the morning while his kids sleep and the birds wake. He lives in Northern California next to a creek he spends a lot of time with. His poetry has been published in *Heart of Flesh, Amethyst Review, Ekstasis, Solid Food Press*, and elsewhere.

MLuv is a dynamic poet, author, writer, speaker and advocate for mental health. She captivated audiences as the creator/host/producer of the acclaimed *Live Life In The Purple Radio Show* (2015-2018) on the IBNXRADIO.COMNetwork. In 2019, she unveiled her first book of poetry, *Thoughts From A Purple Mind*, accompanied by the *Sounds From A Purple Mind* CD. She is the CEO of Purple Door Creations, LLC. Her name, pronounced (EM LOVE), was chosen to symbolize her enduring quest for self-love, empowering her to overcome years of inner struggles. When she's not writing, Mluv indulges in chasing rainbows, savoring mesmerizing sunsets and daydreaming in poetry.

Ebony Patiño discovered poetry in the classrooms of Chemistry and Literature in high school where she drew inspiration to write. Her first performance occurred at Center stage in Baltimore, Maryland where she along with other creatives constructed a unique themed show incorporating spoken word. She has experience in songwriting, is currently a Neuroscience student at Georgia State University and completing her first novel.

Jennifer O'Neill Pickering is an award winning literary and visual artist. Her prose and poetry are published in print, audio and online nationwide. Her poem *I Am the Creek* was selected for the site-specific sculpture, *Open Circle* an art in public places project in Sacramento, CA. Jennifer's latest poetry book, *Fruit Box Castles: Poems from a Peach Rancher's Daughter* is available from Finishing Line Press.
Recent publications include prose in *Persimmon Tree*, and poetry in *California Quarterly*, *Moonstone Press*, and *Tule Review*. A little-known fact about Jennifer is that she once danced with Allen Ginsburg.

Shawn Pittard is the author of three slender volumes of poetry: *Witness*, forthcoming, was a finalist in The Poetry Box 2024 chapbook contest; *Standing in the River*, which was the winner of Tebot Bach's 2010 Clockwise Chapbook Competition; and *These Rivers* from Rattlesnake Press. He's been a coach for Poetry Out Loud and a California Poet in the Schools, taught recitation and writing in middle schools and high schools, including juvenile hall (yep, they're good kids), as well as with veterans and the men in Folsom Prison. By day, he labored in the field of environmental protection, planning, and public policy, focused on energy.

Danyen Powell was born and lives in Sacramento, California. He mainly writes sparse, image-driven poems and believes in reading as many of the great poets from around the world as he can find. He's been published in a variety of small presses and has had two chapbooks published by Rattlesnake Press. In 2014 he self-published a full-length book of poems called *Words Die Of Thirst*. It's in both English and Spanish (translated by Roberto Knorr). He has attended the Sacramento

Poetry Center's Tuesday night workshop for over 29 years and is the current facilitator for the workshop.

Norman Ross Powers goes by 'Ross' and is eighty-one years of age. He started writing poems in an intentional way about five years ago when he joined a poetry-based support group for caregivers of dementia sufferers. His poems come from a collection written while caring for his wife, Michela. He is interested in the work of Philip Levine, Adrienne Rich, Janice N. Harrington and Francesca Bell. He currently lives alone in a nice home in a nice suburban neighborhood in South Sacramento.

Rick Rayburn has lived in Altadena, Arcata on Humboldt Bay, and Sacramento. He began work at the Coastal Commission as a redwood ecologist, then as a land preservationist at California State Parks. Now retired, he moved from environmental protection to writing, beginning with an eco-poetry class in 2015. His collection, *Under the Overstory*, was published by Random Lane Press in 2020, which also published his second collection, *Slack Tide*, in 2023.

Sandra Rendig was born and grew up in the small town of Sonora, California, a rural land of hills, trees and creeks. The natural world remains a strong influence in her writing, especially the beauty and emotional impact of changing seasons. Now that she's 77 years old, several poems reflect the passing of her own seasons. After a 30-year career teaching young children, she's been writing poetry for self-exploration, joy and solace. She and her husband enjoy bird-watching, kayaking, cooking, and spending time with family and friends.

Melinda Moore Rivasplata holds a B.A. degree in Environmental Biology. Her professional career included work in environmental education, resource management, and environmental planning. Her poems have appeared in *Late Peaches* 2012, *Cosumnes River Journal* 2017, and *Tule Review* 2023. She is the author of the poetry collection *Door With A Heart*.

Yuriy Serebriansky is a Kazakhstani author of Polish origin, literary translator, and cultural researcher. His prose, poetry, and non-fiction have appeared in Kazakh, Russian, Polish, Swiss, American, Czech, Chilean, British literary journals and anthologies and has been translated into several languages. In 2010 and 2014, he was awarded the Russkaya Premia literary award; in 2017, his *Kazakhstani Fairy Tales* was recognized as the best bilingual book for a young audience at the Silk Road Book Fair. His most recent collection, *Trams follow the schedule,* appeared in Kiyev, Ukraine in 2024. **Ariadna Linn**, who translated his poem, is a poet, writer, and translator from Almaty, Kazakstan. She holds a bachelor's degree in World Literature and Language,

Allegra Jostad Silberstein grew up on a farm in Wisconsin but has lived in California since 1963. Her love of poetry began as a child...her mother would recite poems as she worked. In addition to two books of poems, she has three chapbooks and has been widely published in journals. Allegra dances and performs with Panela Trokanski's Third Stage Company. She also sings with the Davis Threshold Choir.

Don Solomon has been writing poetry since middle school. His first poems were published in Scholastic Magazine when he was a high school senior. He was a first-grade teacher and literacy trainer for 32 years. He lives in Vacaville with his wife, Andrea and dog, Zoey.

Bob Stanley studied poetry at Caltech and UCLA, and taught English and Creative Writing at Solano College, Sacramento City College, and Sacramento State before retiring in 2021. President of Sacramento Poetry Center for 12 years, Bob has organized hundreds of poetry events, and served as Sacramento Poet Laureate from 2009 to 2012. His poetry collections include *Walt Whitman Orders a Cheeseburger* (Rattlesnake Press, 2009), *Eleven Blue Strings* (little m press, 2012), *Miracle Shine* (CW Books, 2013) and the e-chapbook *November Sun* (Random Lane Press, 2022). Bob lives in Sacramento with his wife, Joyce Hsiao, and they run online poetry seminars that help support small nonprofits. His newest collection of poems, *Language Barrier,* was published by CW Books in June 2024.

Jeanine Stevens' fifth collection, *Left Handed Humming Bird,* will be released by Clare Songbirds Publishing, 2024. Her latest chapbook is *Tea in the Nun's Library*, (Eyewear Publishing, UK, 2022). *Gertrude Sitting: Portraits of Women* won the Heartland Review Chapbook Contest. Jeanine has been published in numerous literary journals, including internationally. Jeanine studied poetry at U.C. Davis, received her M.A. at CSU Sacramento and has a doctorate in Education. She is Professor Emerita at American River College. Raised in Indiana, she now lives with her husband Greg Chalpin in Northern California.

Alex Stolis lives in Minneapolis; he has had poems published in numerous journals. Two full length collections *Pop. 1280,* and *John Berryman Died Here* were released by Cyberwit and available on Amazon. His work has previously appeared or is forthcoming in *Piker's Press, Jasper's Folly Poetry Journal, Beatnik Cowboy,* and elsewhere. His chapbook, *Postcards from the Knife-Thrower's Wife,* was released by Louisiana Literature Press in 2024. *RIP Winston Smith* is forthcoming from Allen Buddha Press. He has been nominated multiple times for the Pushcart Prize.

Gary Thomas grew up on a peach farm outside Empire, California. Prior to retirement, he taught eighth grade language arts and junior college English. His poems have been published or accepted for publication in *The Comstock Review, MockingHeart Review, Atticus* Review, *River Heron Review, Barzakh,* and *The Banyan Review* among others, and in the anthology *More Than Soil, More Than Sky: The Modesto Poets.* He is a founding member of the Modesto-Stanislaus Poetry Center (MoSt) and of the Stanislaus County writing group known as The Licensed Fools. A full-length collection, *All the Connecting Lights,* was released in August 2022 from Finishing Line Press.

Ziaeddin Torabi is an Iranian American poet living in Sacramento. He holds a B.A. in English & Literature and an M.A.in Linguistics from Iranian Universities. Tobari has published more than 30 books of poetry, criticisms, reviews, and translations (in Iran). He won the 2010 Iran Annual Book Prize for his poetry collection, *Face To Face With Dream* which was translated into English by Parisa Samady and published by Ad Luman press, Sacramento, in 2015. His most recent book, *Birds of Imagination and other Poems,* was published by Amazon (2020).

Cover artist **Donna D. Vitucci** has been publishing since 1990. She lives in North Carolina, where she enjoys reading and writing, yoga, hiking, cooking and gardening. Dozens of her stories, poems and slices of memoir can be found in print and online. Her work explores the ache and mistake of secrets among family, lovers and friends. Read selected publications, and information about her four novels, at: www.magicmasterminds.com/donnavitucci. She is a member of Alamance Artisans Guild, and her work can be viewed at: Donna D. Vitucci | Alamance Artisans Guild.

Ann Wehrman is a creative writer and musician living in Sacramento, CA. Her writing has appeared in print and online journals, including *Tule Review, Medusa's Kitchen*, the *Voices* anthologies from Cold River Press, *Blue Heron Review*, and *First Literary Review-East*. Ann teaches English composition online for the University of Phoenix and the University of Arizona Global Campus. She can also be found playing flute, practicing yoga, reading, and cooking.

Patricia J. Wentzel has been writing poetry for about nine years as part of her recovery from a Bipolar Disorder episode. She and her family live in Sacramento, CA. Her calico cat, Margie, helped her write this bio. She has been published in the *Journal of American Medical Association, The Light Exphrastic, Poetry Now, Muse, The Voices Project*, and elsewhere. Her life as a poet has been nurtured by the Women's Wisdom Art program, the Sacramento Prose and Poetry Meetup, and Sacramento Poetry Center members.

Wendy Patrice Williams is the author of the poetry collection *In Chaparral: Life on the Georgetown Divide, California* (Cold River Press) and two chapbooks: *Some New Forgetting* and *Bayley House Bard*. Her memoir, *Autobiography of a Sea Creature: Healing the Trauma of Infant Surgery*, was recently published by the University of California Health Humanities Press. Besides hiking the trails of southern Oregon, you can find her at https://www.wendywilliamsauthor.org.

Nanci Woody was a college professor, textbook author, and Dean of Business before writing her first novel, *Tears and Trombones*, which won several awards. She has published many short stories and poems in print anthologies as well as in online journals. She has completed the pilot to convert *Tears and Trombones* to an eight-episode streaming series.

Andrena Zawinski's four full-length books of poetry, smaller collections, and book of flash fiction have been praised for social concern and spirituality, free verse, and form. Her latest book of poetry is *Born Under the Influence*. She has been a featured reader for Sacramento Poetry Center and contributor to *Tule Review*.

Stan Zumbiel taught English in middle and high school for thirty-five years and has had a hand in raising four children. In 2008 he received his MFA in Writing from Vermont College of Fine Arts. He has published two books: *Standing Watch* from Random Lane Press and *Hat Full of Leaves* from Cold River Press.

ABOUT THE EDITORS

Editor **Linda Jackson Collins** has been writing and editing in the Sacramento community for over 10 years. Her collection, *Painting Trees*, published by Random Lane Press, won the Gold Medal in poetry from Northern California Publishers and Authors (NCPA) in its 2019 contest. In addition, she has had individual poems published in numerous literary journals. Learn more at www.ljcreviews.com

Managing editor **Patrick Grizzell** is a founding editor of *Tule Review*, and serves as president of The Sacramento Poetry Center.

Made in the USA
Columbia, SC
15 February 2025